Ballerina Girl

Written by Kirsten Hall

Illustrated by Anne Kennedy

My First
READER

children's press ®

A Division of Scholastic Inc.
New York Toronto London Auckland Sydney
Mexico City New Delhi Hong Kong
Danbury, Connecticut

Library of Congress Cataloging-in-Publication Data

Hall, Kirsten.
  Ballerina girl / written by Kirsten Hall ; illustrated by Anne
Kennedy.– 1st American ed.
      p. cm. – (My first reader)
Summary: A little girl puts on different costumes and pretends she's a
ballerina performing for an audience.
  ISBN 0-516-22921-4 (lib. bdg.)   0-516-24623-2 (pbk.)
  [1. Ballet dancing–Fiction. 2. Imagination–Fiction. 3. Stories in
rhyme.] I. Kennedy, Anne, 1955- ill. II. Title. III. Series.
  PZ8.3.H146Bal 2003
  [E]–dc21
                                    2003003635

Note to Parents and Teachers

Once a reader can recognize and identify the 33 words
used to tell this story, he or she will be able to read successfully
the entire book. These 33 words are repeated throughout the story,
so that young readers will be able to easily recognize
the words and understand their meaning.

The 33 words used in this book are:

a	for	sky	you
can	I'm	tippy	bows
fly	pink	with	do
I	tie	ballet	hair
on	twirl	day	my
the	ballerina	gown	star
tutu	dance	like	
all	girl	spin	
crown	in	toes	

I'm a ballerina girl.

I can spin. I can twirl.

I can do a dance for you.

Do you like my pink tutu?

I can dance on tippy toes!

I can dance! I can fly!

Ballerina in the sky!

Ballerina in a gown.

Ballerina with a crown.

I can dance for you all day.

I'm the star in my ballet!

I can spin. I can twirl.

I'm a ballerina girl.